POP GOES THE CIRCUS!
GOU
Deliver trainload of
private peanut farm.
RUSH ORDER
Acme Circus Balloons
Sir Sidney's Circus: 1,000 more balloons
CANCEL ORDER
APPEARING FRIDAY NIGHT ONLY!
Veronica Twist and Squeaky
Show starts promptly at 7:00
Tickets $3
No refunds. No guarantees. Caveat emptor.
THE DIARY OF BERT
My name is Bert. I am a mouse.
This is my story.

THIS BOOK
BELONGS TO:

OTHER BOOKS WRITTEN BY **KATE KLISE** AND ILLUSTRATED BY **M. SARAH KLISE**

Three-Ring Rascals
The Show Must Go On!
The Greatest Star on Earth
The Circus Goes to Sea

43 Old Cemetery Road
Dying to Meet You
Over My Dead Body
Till Death Do Us Bark
The Phantom of the Post Office
Hollywood, Dead Ahead
Greetings from the Graveyard
The Loch Ness Punster

Regarding the Fountain
Regarding the Sink
Regarding the Trees
Regarding the Bathrooms
Regarding the Bees

Letters from Camp
Trial by Journal

Shall I Knit You a Hat?
Why Do You Cry?
Imagine Harry
Little Rabbit and the Night Mare
Little Rabbit and the Meanest Mother on Earth
Stand Straight, Ella Kate
Grammy Lamby and the Secret Handshake

BOOK 4

Three-Ring Rascals

POP GOES the CIRCUS!

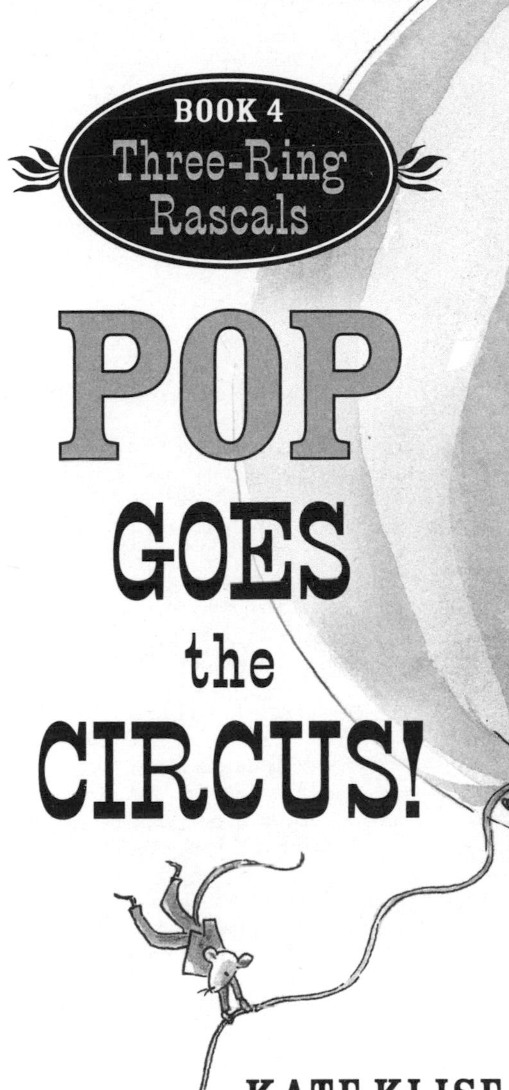

KATE KLISE

ILLUSTRATED BY

M. SARAH KLISE

ALGONQUIN YOUNG READERS • 2015

Published by
ALGONQUIN YOUNG READERS
an imprint of Algonquin Books of Chapel Hill
Post Office Box 2225
Chapel Hill, North Carolina 27515-2225

a division of
Workman Publishing
225 Varick Street
New York, New York 10014

Printed in the United States of America.
Published simultaneously in Canada by Thomas Allen & Son Limited.
Design by M. Sarah Klise.

Library of Congress Cataloging-in-Publication Data
Klise, Kate.
Pop goes the circus! / Kate Klise ; illustrated by M. Sarah Klise.
pages cm.—(Three-ring rascals : book 4)
Summary: A misbehaving mouse, under the employ of Sir Sidney's Circus, finds adventure when a balloon carries him away and he meets a young runaway.
ISBN 978-1-61620-464-8
[1. Mice—Fiction. 2. Circus—Fiction. 3. Behavior—Fiction. 4. Runaways—Fiction. 5. Adventure and adventurers—Fiction.] I. Klise, M. Sarah, illustrator. II. Title.
PZ7.K684Po 2015
[Fic]—dc23 2014043004

10 9 8 7 6 5 4 3 2 1
First Edition

This book is dedicated to
the memory of our pop,
Thomas S. Klise.

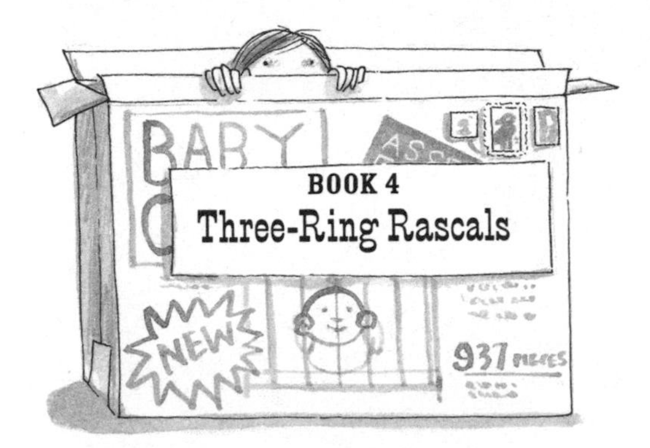
BABY
BOOK 4
Three-Ring Rascals
NEW
937

POP
GOES
the
CIRCUS!

Not till we are lost . . .
do we begin to find ourselves.
—Henry David Thoreau

CHAPTER ONE

"Bert," said Gert. There was no answer.

"Bert!" she said in a louder voice. Still no answer.

"Bertrand!" Gert yelled as loud as she could. It was her brother's real name, though she used it only when she was frustrated.

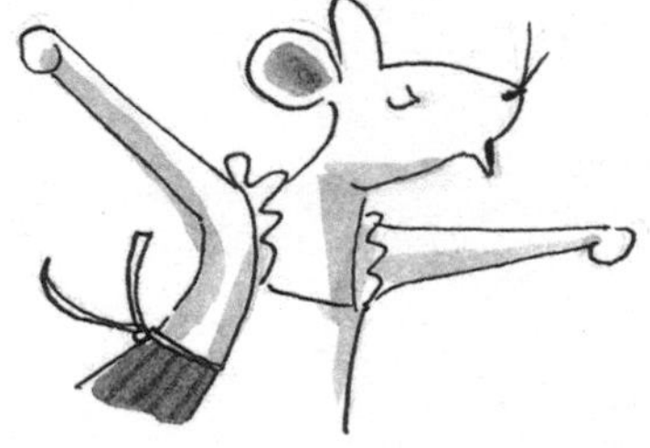

Bert and Gert were the smallest members of Sir Sidney's Circus. Years ago, Sir Sidney had found them on his circus train. They were just babies then, or *pinkies,* as newborn mice are called.

Sir Sidney gave them food, clothes, and a comfortable mouse hole to live in. He even invited Bert and Gert to join his traveling circus. Their job was to clean up the spilled popcorn left after every show.

Gert took her job seriously. She never missed a show. Bert, on the other hand, was not nearly as reliable as his sister. When it was time for chores, he liked to hide. This is why Gert was feeling frustrated.

Gert decided to ask her friends for help. She began with Elsa the elephant.

In addition to dancing in the circus, Elsa was responsible for making sure everyone in Sir Sidney's Circus took a bath on Sunday night.

"Elsa, do you know where Bert is?" Gert asked.

"I don't," said Elsa. "He was supposed to take his bath at eight o'clock tonight. But it's eight thirty and his tub is still full."

Gert scurried off to the dining car, where she found Leo and Tiger mopping the floor. The friendly felines were terrific singers. They also did a fine job keeping the circus train tidy.

Have you seen my brother?

“Mrrare,” said Tiger the kitten, shaking her head.

“Neither have I,” said Leo the lion. “Bert was supposed to clear the table after dinner tonight. I guess he forgot.”

Gert spent the next twenty minutes carrying dishes from the table to the sink so Leo and Tiger could wash and dry them.

Gert then climbed up to the roof of the sleeping car. She knew she'd find the Famous Flying Banana Brothers there, practicing tricks on their trapeze.

"Not since this afternoon," said Stan Banana.

"He asked to borrow something," said Dan Banana.

"We'd help you look for Bert," said Stan Banana, "but we have work to do."

"Look at all these balloons we have to blow up for tomorrow's show," said Dan Banana. "You should ask Old Coal where Bert is."

"Good idea!" said Gert. "Old Coal can find anyone in the whole wide world."

But Old Coal had a headache.

Finally, Gert decided to ask Sir Sidney. She found him in his office. He was making a poster for the next show.

Gert watched Sir Sidney work. He was the nicest man she had ever known. He was also responsible, reliable, and predictable—unlike her brother.

"Sir Sidney," said Gert, "I have a problem."

"Tell me," said Sir Sidney. "I'm sure we can think of a solution, whatever the problem is."

"The problem isn't a *what,*" said Gert. "It's a *who.* Bert. He's hiding from me because he hasn't been doing his chores. *I* had to clean up all the spilled popcorn after this afternoon's show in Minneapolis. *And* I cleared the dinner table. It's not fair."

Sir Sidney bent down to speak to Gert.

“Do you remember when I bought you a typewriter? I gave it to you because I thought you’d like it.”

“*Like* it?” said Gert. “I *love* my typewriter. I’ve had so much fun using it to write letters and stories.”

“I’m glad,” said Sir Sidney, smiling. “But I decided today that I should give something special to Bert to encourage him to write, too.”

“What did you give him?” asked Gert eagerly.

“A diary,” said Sir Sidney. “It’s small enough to fit in his pocket. I wonder if he’s spent the day writing in it.”

Now Gert smiled. “That would explain a lot of things. Bert is easily distracted, especially when it comes to doing chores.”

“I’ll make sure Bert does his chores tomorrow and helps you with yours, too,” said Sir Sidney. “Does that sound fair?”

“Yes,” said Gert. “Thank you.”

As she left Sir Sidney's office, Gert was in a much better mood than she'd been in an hour earlier. She wondered what her brother was writing in his diary.

Whatever Bert writes, I'm *sure* it will be funny.

Inside the mouse hole, Gert saw her brother's tail poking out from under his bed. She could hear the sound of muffled laughter and pages turning. Bert's tail twitched every time he laughed.

"Reading something funny?" Gert asked slyly.

"Huh?" answered the voice from under the bed. "I mean, uh, yeah."

"Do you think *I'd* like to read it?" Gert continued.

"Uh-huh," said the voice.

"Care to share?" pressed Gert. She was itching to know what her brother was writing in his new diary.

But Bert answered with only a gurgle and a giggle.

"Will you *please* come out from under there?" Gert pleaded.

Bert's head appeared from under the bed.

"Of course," said Gert, "after you tell me about your day. I hear you received a nice surprise."

"I'll say," said Bert. He slid a stack of comic books toward Gert. "I never thought the Famous Flying Banana Brothers would lend me *seven* of their best comic books."

"Comic books?" said Gert.

"Yeah," said Bert. "And they let me borrow this book, too. It's called *How to Whistle.* I can't wait to learn."

Gert was confused. "But what about your new diary?"

Bert scooted out from under the bed. "You mean *this* thing?" he asked, pulling the diary from his pocket.

It's a book filled with blank pages. What am I supposed to do with it?
You can fill a diary with your deep thoughts and thrilling secrets.

Bert thought for a moment. "I don't *have* any deep thoughts or thrilling secrets."

"Then write a little every day about the exciting tidbits of your life," suggested Gert.

"Exciting tidbits?" repeated Bert. "My life doesn't have any *exciting tidbits.*" He tossed the book to Gert and then flung his tiny legs in the air so that he was standing on his paws. "My life today is the same as it was yesterday. Why waste time writing anything in a boring old diary?"

Why can't you just be good and do what Sir Sidney asks you to do?

"Because I'd rather be bad and do what *I* want to do," Bert replied.

"Do you know who you remind me of?" asked Gert. She pointed at two paintings hanging in the mouse hole.

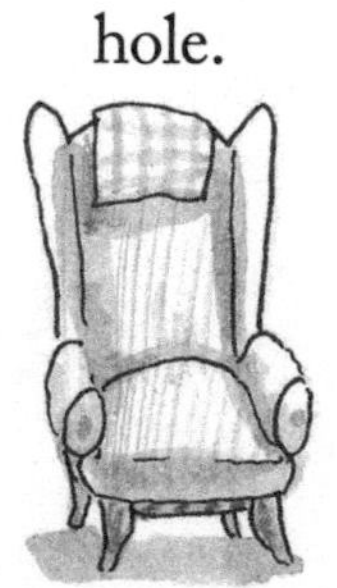

The last time anyone in Sir Sidney's Circus had seen Barnabas Brambles was eight months earlier at his wedding to Astrid LaPasta. No one could believe what a good man he had become. When he joined the circus, Barnabas Brambles was known as the meanest man alive. But Sir Sidney had a generous heart. He was willing to give even a first-class scoundrel like Barnabas Brambles a second chance.

"*I* remind you of *Barnabas Brambles?*" asked Bert.

"Yes," said Gert. "Your *baditude* is similar to Barnabas Brambles's *baditude* when we first met him. He's much nicer now."

"Fine," said Bert. "I know when I'm not wanted." He left the mouse hole without looking back.

Bert decided to spend the night on top of the sleeping car, learning to whistle. He found a quiet place where he could read *How to Whistle* by the light of the moon.

Bert opened the book and read the first page out loud. “First, lick your lips.” Bert licked his lips. “Next, press lips together to form a small circle, as if saying the letter *O*.” Bert did as the book suggested. “Now, curl tongue slightly and blow out a steady stream of air.”

Nothing. Bert had followed the instructions, but he wasn’t whistling. He kept reading. “If at first you don’t succeed, keep trying. Learning to whistle takes practice.”

He tried again.

And again.

And again.

"This is impossible," Bert grumbled. "I'll never learn how to whistle." He decided to try one last time.

He *did* it. He whistled! He kept his lips just as they were and kept blowing. He was whistling! He couldn't believe his ears.

Bert threw the book aside and continued whistling. He drew air in and blew it out. Both methods produced pleasant sounds, like two birds calling to each other. Bert didn't pause to take a breath. He was afraid if he did, he might forget how to get his lips back in the whistling position.

The more Bert whistled, the happier he became. He was also getting a bit dizzy from not breathing. He grabbed hold of a balloon string to steady himself.

Bert had never felt so proud of himself. *He could whistle!* His heart soared. He closed his eyes and held on tightly, not realizing how loosely Stan and Dan Banana had tied the knot on the ballon string.

I'm so happy, I feel like I could fly.

And then he *was* flying. The loose knot had slipped. Carried upward by a balloon, Bert was floating over the circus train, drifting farther and farther from the only home he had ever known.

Nobody knew he was gone.

CHAPTER TWO

On that same Sunday evening, a ten-year-old girl was writing a letter on a ship named the SS *Spaghetti*.

Flora Endora Eliza LaBuena LaPasta
Aboard the SS *Spaghetti*

July 27

Sir Sidney and Friends
c/o Sir Sidney's Circus
Somewhere in the USA

Dear Friends,

I miss you! It seems like forever since you came to visit me aboard the SS *Spaghetti*. Who would've guessed that Barnabas Brambles would fall in love with my mother, or that they'd get married? Did you know Barnabas Brambles adopted me after the wedding? Well, he did. He's really nice and funny now. And guess what else? Our family is going to have a baby. Isn't that exciting? The only problem is

Flora stopped writing. How could she explain the problem? She stood up from her desk and went in search of her mother.

She found Captain Astrid Amanda Miranda LaBuena LaPasta at the helm of the *Spaghetti*.

Mom, when can I go visit Sir Sidney's Circus?

"Hmm?" said her pregnant mother as she stared into the distance.

"Remember how we agreed that I'd visit our friends at Sir Sidney's Circus once a year?" said Flora. "Well, in a few months it will be a whole year since we've seen them. Can we please plan my visit to the circus?"

Her mother rubbed her belly. "I'm sorry, dear. I have a lot on my mind right now. Go ask your father."

Flora found Barnabas Brambles in the ship's nursery. He was trying to assemble a baby crib.

He was busy reading the instructions.

How to Assemble a Baby Crib

1. Find piece #207-B.

2. Nail piece #204-C to piece #403-X.

3. Throw away piece #207-B.

4. Cut piece #721-J in half while whistling "Yankee Doodle."

5. Turn a cartwheel while inserting slot A into tab B.

6. 祝你今天愉快!

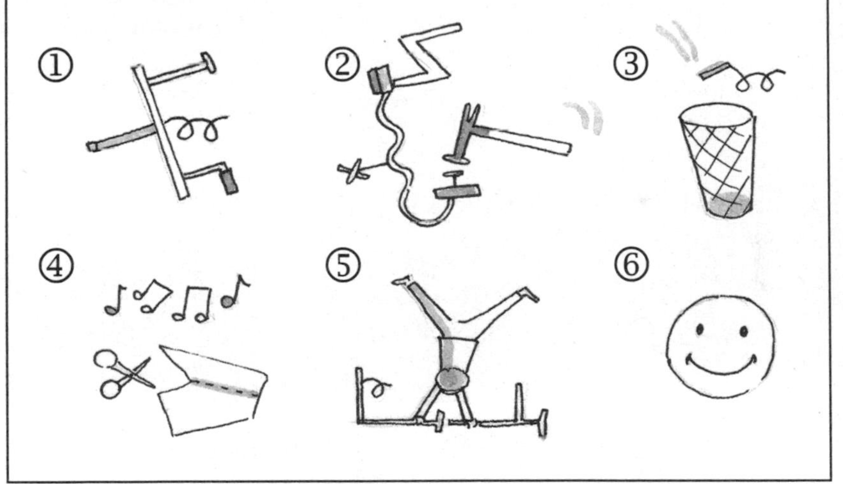

"You and Mom said I could go," Flora continued.

"Go where?" mumbled Barnabas Brambles.

"I want to visit my friends at Sir Sidney's Circus," Flora said. "Next week might be a good time. Or maybe next month?"

Barnabas Brambles looked up from the instructions. “This is a busy time for our family, Flora. We’re going to be even busier next month when the baby arrives. Look at all the things we’ll have to do.” He handed her a baby book.

Chapter One

To care for a new baby, you must do the following every day:

Feed baby

Bathe baby

Burp baby

Read to baby

Rock baby to sleep

Take pictures of baby

Change baby’s diapers

Admire baby

Obey baby

“But what about *me*?” asked Flora. “When will we do the things *I* want to do, like visit Sir Sidney’s Circus?”

But Barnabas Brambles wasn't listening. He was still trying to make sense of the crib instructions. "This is impossible," he grumbled.

"Yes it is," said Flora. And she wasn't talking about the baby crib.

She turned on her heel to leave but stopped when she saw the empty box for the crib. An idea began to take shape in her mind. She looked at the calendar on the wall.

BABY CRIB
Are we going to dock in Miami tomorrow?
Yes. It's a good thing, too, because I need to mail this crib back to the factory.

"I could do that for you," Flora offered.

"Would you?" asked Barnabas Brambles. "Gee, that would be terrific! You're going to be a *big* help when the baby arrives. Here's twenty dollars for the postage."

Flora took the money and smiled. She then helped Barnabas Brambles load the crib parts into the box.

But the next day when Flora went to the Miami post office, she didn't mail the box to the crib factory. Instead, she removed the wooden pieces and crawled into the box.

She mailed herself to Sir Sidney's Circus.

CHAPTER THREE

On Sunday night, the balloon carried Bert over Minnesota. During the next three days, he flew over Iowa, Illinois, Kentucky, and Tennessee.

He ate nothing and drank only the rain that fell on Thursday morning. It was his fourth day away from home.

"I don't know how much longer I can live like this," Bert said to himself. He was hungry and tired, but he worried that if he fell asleep he would let go of the balloon and fall. He had never felt so alone. It was the worst day of his life.

Bert was cold and damp. He gazed up at the balloon, and then looked down at the ground. The view made him woozy. He tried to cheer himself up by whistling, but he couldn't make the *O* shape with his lips. Being far from home and afraid made his mouth look like an upside-down *U.* A tiny tear was forming in the corner of one eye. Soon he was crying.

“I can’t hold on to this balloon forever!” cried Bert. “This is the end. I’ll never see Gert again or Sir Sidney or Tiger or Leo or Elsa or Old Coal or the Famous Flying Banana Brothers. I’ll never read another comic book or make up a joke or eat hot buttered pop—”

But before he could finish his sentence, he heard a loud noise.

A sharp branch from an apple tree had punctured the balloon. Bert fell into the tree. He stayed still for a moment, unsure if he was dead or alive.

Slowly, Bert examined his body. One knee was sore. Both arms were scratched. Other than that, he was okay.

Bert made a bandage out of a leaf and wrapped it around his sore knee. Luckily, he still had the balloon string. He used his sharp teeth to bite off a short piece, which he tied around the leaf to keep it in place. Then he stood up and brushed himself off.

As he did, he heard a man talking. The voice was coming from a mail truck below. Bert jumped from the tree onto the roof of the truck to listen.

"Somewhere in the USA," the man said angrily into a phone. "What kind of an address is *that*? I can't deliver a package without knowing the street number, city, state, and zip code." He paused. "No, I can't do *that,* either. There's no return address. Huh? Really? There's a warehouse for this stuff? Right here in Mobile, Alabama? Okay, I'll take the package there."

The mail truck started to move. Thinking fast, Bert tied what remained of the balloon string around his waist and threw the opposite end around the rearview mirror.

Bert was grateful to know where he was. “Mobile, Alabama,” he said to himsclf. “I’m *mobile* in Mobile.” Any other time he might have laughed at the coincidence. At the moment, he was too busy trying to stay alivc.

Five minutes later, the truck arrived at a warehouse for undeliverable mail. The driver jumped out of the vehicle, grabbed the package, and tossed it onto a loading dock. “Here’s one addressed to Sir Sidney’s Circus!” he yelled with a laugh. “Somewhere in the USA.”

Bert quickly untied the string from his waist. He took a running leap and swung on the string as if it were a jungle vine. He landed on the loading dock just as the mail truck pulled away from the warehouse.

Bert took a deep breath. He climbed on top of the box to rest. Suddenly, he heard a voice coming from inside the box.

Bert jumped off.

“Hello, hello,” the voice repeated. “Whoever you are, can you help me get out, please?”

“Sure,” Bert said. “Give me a second to open this box.”

He looked around for tools. "I need something sharp to rip the tape," Bert said. He was talking to himself, but the voice inside the box answered.

"Do you have long fingernails?"

Bert looked at his claws. "You could say that," he said. "I also have sharp teeth."

Using his claws and teeth, Bert successfully opened the box. Out popped Flora.

"I can't believe it," said Flora, hugging Bert. "Did you run away from home, too?"

"No," said Bert. "I *flew* away on a balloon, but I didn't mean to."

Now that he thought about it, though, Bert couldn't believe his good luck. Of course he loved Sir Sidney and the circus. But he *didn't* love taking baths or clearing the table after dinner. He *didn't* love having to say "Pretty please with bananas on top" when he wanted to borrow a comic book from the Famous Flying Banana Brothers. Most of all, he *didn't* love being told he had a *baditude* by Gert, who was always as good as gold and never got into trouble.

"Hot diggity dog!" Bert said. "This is the best day of my life. I'll never have to take another bath or clear the dishes from the table."

"I'll never have to burp a baby or change a stinky diaper," said Flora.

"I'll never have to keep a diary," said Bert, "or clean up after the show by eating leftover popcorn." He stopped. His stomach was growling. "Are you hungry?"

"Famished," said Flora. "But I didn't pack any food. Did you?"

"Nope," admitted Bert. "There's an apple tree a mile or so that way." He pointed in the direction of the tree that had popped his balloon.

Thirty minutes later, Flora and Bert were sitting on a park bench, eating apples.

"These apples aren't ripe," said Flora, "but they'll fill us up. Wouldn't it be nice to have peanut butter to spread on them?"

"Mmmm," agreed Bert while chewing. "Popcorn is also good with apples. If we had money, we could buy peanut butter *and* popcorn. Some lemonade would be nice, too." He paused to chew. "I didn't bring any money. Did you?"

"Yes," said Flora. "I had twenty dollars, but I spent nineteen dollars and ninety-eight cents at the post office."

Bert did the math problem in his head.

"That means you have only two cents left," Bert said. "Hmm. Maybe we should get jobs."

"Excellent idea!" Flora said, jumping to her feet. "Let's open a circus. I'd love to be a clown."

Bert frowned and rubbed his stomach. The unripe apples were already giving him a bellyache. "We need more than a clown and a mouse to be a circus."

"We could put on a play," Flora suggested. "We'll sell tickets to see it."

"I'm not good at memorizing lines," said Bert.

"What *are* you good at doing?" asked Flora.

"I can whistle," said Bert. He climbed onto Flora's knee and began to whistle an old song called "Oh! Susanna." Flora knew the words and sang along.

I come from Alabama
With my banjo on my knee,
I'm going to Louisiana
My true love for to see.

It rained all night the day I left,
The weather it was dry.
The sun so hot I froze to death,
Susanna, don't you cry.

(Chorus)
Oh! Susanna,
Oh don't you cry for me,
For I come from Alabama
With my banjo on my knee.

As Flora sang and Bert whistled, a buzz of excitement surrounded them. People were gathering to watch and listen.

Is that *her*?
It must be. And that's *him*. How exciting!
Where can we buy tickets? I'd like three, please.
I need four tickets.

"Look at all the people," Bert whispered to Flora. "They must really like that song."

A woman with red lipstick pushed through the crowd. "It's such an honor to meet you in person, Veronica," the woman said to Flora. She turned to Bert. "It's a thrill to meet you, too, Squeaky."

"Huh?" said Bert.

Flora looked at the woman. "I'm sorry, but I think you've mistaken us for somebody—"

Before Flora could finish, the woman handed Flora a poster. "Would you autograph this for me? Just write your name under your picture."

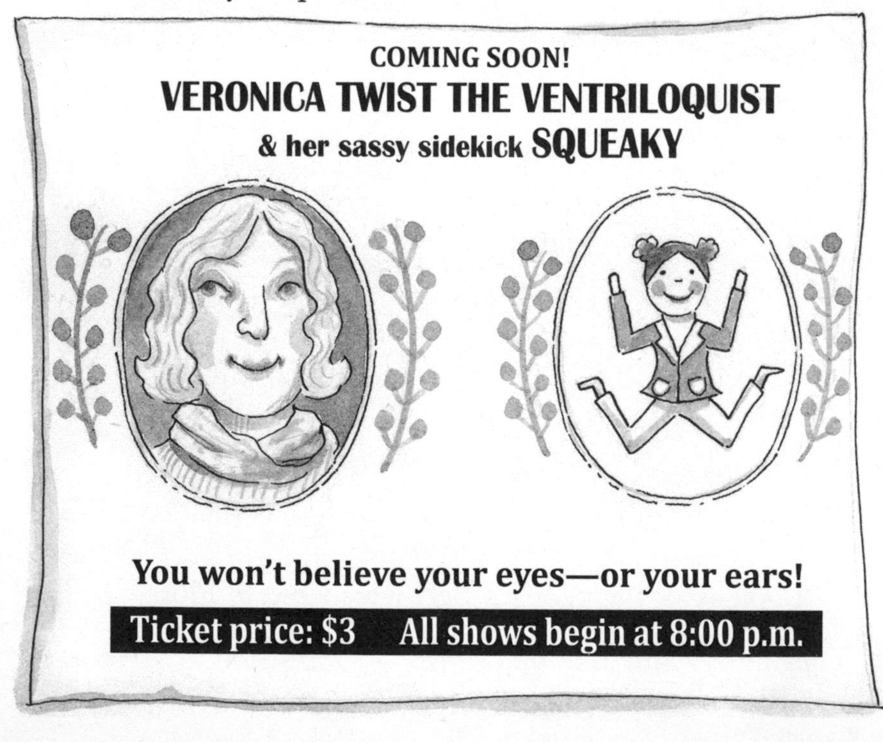

COMING SOON!
VERONICA TWIST THE VENTRILOQUIST
& her sassy sidekick SQUEAKY
You won't believe your eyes—or your ears!
Ticket price: $3
All shows begin at 8:00 p.m.

"I saw your show last year in Chicago," the woman with red lipstick said to Flora. "I never saw your mouth move, Veronica. It *really* looked like your little Squeaky puppet could *talk.*" She reached over to pat Bert on the head.

"Now look here, lady," Bert said. "My name is *not* Squeaky, and I am *not* a puppet."

The crowd laughed and cheered.

Flora whispered in Bert's ear. "These people think you're a puppet and I'm a famous ventriloquist named Veronica Twist."

"What's a *ventriloquist*?" Bert asked quietly.

"A ventriloquist is an entertainer who works with a puppet," explained Flora. "Ventriloquists can talk without moving their lips. They use a string to move the puppet's mouth. To the audience, it looks like the puppet is talking, not the ventriloquist."

"And that's what they think *we're* doing?" asked Bert.

"Yes," Flora whispered. "I agree it's very strange. But Bert, this could be our *job*. We could make money to buy peanut butter."

"And popcorn," Bert said.

Flora nodded. "And lemonade, too. What do you think?"

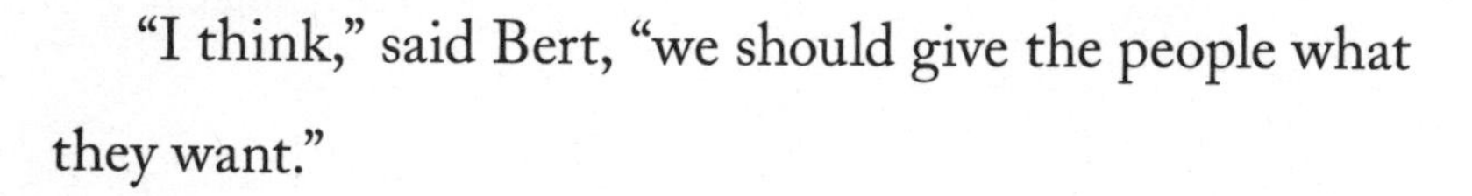

"I think," said Bert, "we should give the people what they want."

Flora stood on the park bench. “Attention, everyone! In thirty minutes, tickets will go on sale for tomorrow night’s show. You won’t want to miss it! See me, Veronica Twist the ventriloquist, and my sidekick, Squeaky. Only three dollars per ticket. The show starts at seven o’clock.”

2 tickets x $3 = $6
3 tickets x $3 = $9
4 tickets x $3 = $12
5 tickets x $3 = $15
500 tickets x $3 =$1,500

Flora and Bert sold five hundred tickets in an hour.

"We just made one thousand five hundred dollars," Flora whispered to Bert. "Now all we have to do is put on a good show."

"We'll practice," said Bert. "We'll be terrific! Everyone will think you're Veronica Twist and I'm Squeaky."

Little did they know the *real* Veronica Twist was in San Francisco, California, boarding a train for Mobile, Alabama. She was scheduled to arrive the following evening at 7:55 with her famous puppet, Squeaky.

CHAPTER FOUR

No one in Sir Sidney's Circus could find Bert. But everyone had a theory about where he was.

Maybe he ran ahead to buy new comic books.
He'll probably meet us at the next stop. You know how Bert is.
I think he might've stayed behind at the last stop to see a movie. You know how Bert is.
Maybe he's playing hide-and-seek. You know how Bert is.
Mrraare.

Gert lifted her tiny paws above her head. "I know *exactly* how Bert is, and I'm telling you he didn't do *any* of those things. He ran away and *it's all my fault.*" Tears rolled down her cheeks and off her whiskers. She was so worried, her brown fur was turning gray.

Sir Sidney kneeled down to talk to Gert. "Why do you think this is your fault, Gert?"

"Because it *is,*" she said, covering her eyes with her paws. "Why did I criticize Bert so harshly? Why did I think it was my job to point out his flaws? We'll never see Bert again, and it's all because of *me.*"

"Don't worry," said Stan Banana. "We'll find him. We put an announcement in the *Circus Times.*"

"We'll get it in every newspaper in the United States," added Dan Banana.

MISSING

Have You Seen This Mouse?

Our friend Bert is gone.
If you have any information about him,
please contact Sir Sidney's Circus.

"It's a good idea," said Sir Sidney. "Let's hope we hear from someone soon."

"But what if we don't?" asked Elsa. "How long can a little mouse survive on his own?"

"I know cats who *eat* mice for breakfast," Leo said darkly.

"Mrraare," agreed Tiger, wiping a tear with her tail.

"I know just how you feel," said Gert. "I have a *saditude,* too."

As they were talking, Old Coal flew in the window. "Aw! Aw!" the black crow cried. She had been searching for Bert for four days.

"Tell us some good news, Old Coal," said Stan Banana.

"We know you can find anyone in the whole wide world," added Dan Banana.

sad + attitude = saditude
Have you found Bert?
Where is he?
Did you bring him home?

Old Coal just shook her head. Searching for Bert had made her headache even worse.

"If Old Coal can't find Bert, *no one* can," cried Gert in despair.

"Let's not give up hope yet," said Sir Sidney. "Old Coal, will you please keep looking?"

"Aw! Aw!" said Old Coal as she flew out the window, bumping her beak on the way.

With a heavy heart, Sir Sidney returned to his office. He took out a pen and wrote a message to his customers.

An Important Message from
Sir Sidney's Circus
We have lost a beloved member
of our circus family.
Until we find him, all scheduled shows
are canceled.
No future shows are planned.

Meanwhile, Barnabas Brambles and Captain LaPasta were at the Miami police station. They were worried sick.

"It's my fault," Barnabas Brambles told the police captain. "I was distracted by a dastardly baby crib. I should've taken the time to really listen to Flora."

"No, it's *my* fault," said Captain LaPasta, her hand on her belly. "I was too busy worrying about the baby. No wonder Flora ran away. She didn't even leave a note. Will we ever see her again?"

We're doing all we can to find your daughter. Search teams are looking high and low for her.
MISSING
WANTED

"There must be something else we can do," said Captain LaPasta.

Barnabas Brambles snapped his fingers. "I've got it! We'll offer a reward."

"How much money do you have?" Captain LaPasta asked her husband.

Barnabas Brambles opened his wallet. "Ten bucks," he said. "How much do you have?"

"One hundred thousand dollars," replied Captain LaPasta. "I'll give it all to whoever finds our daughter."

So Barnabas Brambles set up a booth.

REWARD
$100,010!
Find our daughter
and the money is yours.

News of the reward traveled fast. Everyone was trying to find the missing ten-year-old girl. Everyone, that is, except two crooks named Buster and Robin. They were interested in one thing only: the money.

"How do we know you really have one hundred thousand ten dollars?" Buster asked Barnabas Brambles.

"You'd better show it to us," Robin said.

Barnabas Brambles piled the money on the table for the crooks to see. A split second later, Buster gave the table a ferocious karate chop while Robin scooped all the money into a bag.

Barnabas Brambles pulled out his phone and sent a text message to the police station.

BB: My wife and I were just robbed.

POLICE: Can you describe what happened?

BB: There were two robbers. One guy busted the table. Another guy stole the money.

POLICE: Sounds like Buster and Robin.

BB: So you know who the robbers are?

POLICE: Yes. They've pulled this trick many times. Buster does the busting while Robin handles the robbing.

BB: Can you catch them and get our money back?

POLICE: Unlikely. Buster and Robin have been on our Most Wanted list for years. We've given up hope of ever catching them.

BB: Oh well. Money doesn't matter as long as we get Flora back.

⇦ ⇨

POLICE: Um . . .

BB: You haven't given up hope of finding Flora, have you?

POLICE: Well . . .

BB: Well, WHAT?

BB: Are you still there?

CONNECTION LOST

Barnabas Brambles turned to Captain LaPasta. His miserable eyes told her the bad news. They had lost their daughter *and* all their money.

Captain LaPasta looked at Barnabas Brambles. She gently patted her belly with one hand. She lifted her other hand to her forehead.

And then she fainted.

CHAPTER FIVE

At six o'clock on Friday night, Flora and Bert were busy selling last-minute tickets.

"It's not too late to buy tickets to tonight's show," Flora said.

Oh good.
I'll take three
tickets, please.

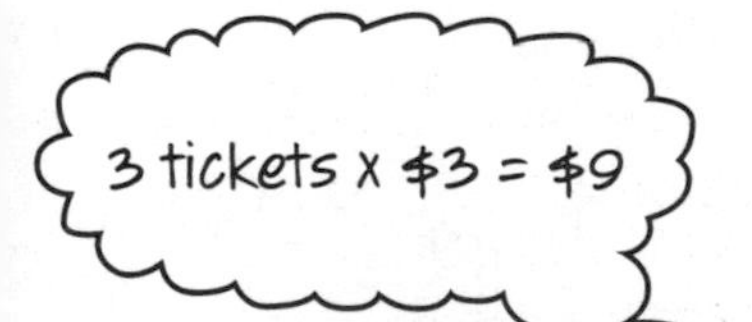

You look so much younger in person, Veronica.
Why, thank you.
Isn't Squeaky cute?
What a doll!
Easy, ladies.
Wouldn't you just love to take him home?

Many people brought picnic baskets to the park. They spread out blankets in the grass and snacked on cheese, crackers, and popcorn before the show. Flora and Bert could smell the tantalizing aromas.

"I'm dying to get my paws on some leftover popcorn," said Bert.

"Me, too," agreed Flora. "But first we have to put on a good show. Now remember, everyone thinks you're a puppet and I'm a famous ventriloquist. We have to make the audience *believe* that."

"No problem," said Bert with confidence. "For the next hour, you're Veronica Twist and I'm Squeaky."

"Good," said Flora. "We'll start the show by thanking everyone for coming. Then we'll tell a few jokes."

"The ones we practiced," said Bert.

"Right," said Flora. "Then I'll sing 'Oh! Susanna' while you whistle the melody."

"And then I'll say, 'Good night, folks,'" said Bert.

"Perfect!" said Flora. "Let's do it."

The show began promptly at seven o'clock. The audience laughed at all the jokes.

For almost an hour, everything went according to plan.

At 7:55 p.m., Veronica Twist arrived at the Mobile station. "Yoo-hoo, taxi!" she cried as she got off the train.

In the taxi, Veronica Twist powdered her nose. Then she used a soft cloth to gently clean Squeaky's face. Even when she was in a hurry, Veronica Twist always took good care of her famous puppet.

Veronica thought about her long career with Squeaky. He had started out years ago as just a piece of wood. As a child, Veronica had carved the wood into a puppet. Audiences loved her puppet, and Veronica loved her audiences. Nothing made her happier than putting on a good show for her fans.

But when Veronica Twist's taxi arrived at the park, she saw her fans enjoying a *different* show. Everyone was watching a young girl sing while something much smaller stood on her lap and whistled.

"That's Veronica Twist the ventriloquist," answered a man. "And that's her sidekick, Squeaky. Aren't they terrific?"

Veronica Twist was shocked. *Someone is pretending to be me and Squeaky,* she thought. She looked at the man. He was holding one of the posters Flora and Bert had made.

APPEARING FRIDAY NIGHT ONLY!
VERONICA TWIST
AND HER SASSY SIDEKICK SQUEAKY
SHOW STARTS PROMPTLY AT 7:00
TICKETS: $3
NO REFUNDS. NO GUARANTEES. CAVEAT EMPTOR.

Veronica Twist marched through the crowd until she was standing directly in front of Flora and Bert. "Of all the nerve!" she said.

"Please sit down," whispered a woman.

"We're trying to see a show," a man said in a louder voice.

"We paid good money to see Veronica Twist," hollered another man.

"I'm sure you did," Veronica Twist said. "But this"—she pointed at Flora—"is *not* Veronica Twist. And that"—she pointed at Bert—"is *not* Squeaky."

"Madam, I'm sorry you missed the show," said Flora. "We were just finishing up. If you'll kindly—"

Veronica Twist interrupted. "Who do you think you are, young lady?"

Flora laughed nervously. "I'm, um, Veronica Twist, of course."

"Really?" said Veronica Twist. "And what's your little friend's name?"

"Everyone knows that's Squishy," said Flora. She was so nervous, she'd forgotten the name of Veronica Twist's puppet.

"She means *Squeaky,*" Bert said. "That's my name."

The audience roared with laughter. Everyone thought it was part of the show.

Veronica Twist took a step closer to Flora and Bert. She glared at the desperate duo. "Which is it?" she demanded. "*Squeaky* or *Squishy*?"

Flora bit her lip. Then she launched into a far-fetched explanation. "*Squishy* is his first name. *Squeaky* is his middle name. Some people call him Squishy. Other people call him Squirmy."

"Squirmy?" said Bert, looking at Flora.

"Ha!" said Veronica Twist, stabbing the air with her finger. "I caught you in your own lie! You're nothing but a fake and a fraud."

"That's not very nice," said Bert.

"*You,*" said Veronica Twist, picking Bert up by the tail, "are nothing but a pip-squeak." She turned to speak to the audience. "Ladies and gentlemen, these performers are impostors. *I* am the real Veronica Twist, and *this* is the real Squeaky." She held the puppet in her other hand for all to see.

"Bert, they're onto us!" Flora said. "What should we do?"

"Run," replied Bert, wriggling out of Veronica's hand. *"RUN!"*

Flora and Bert ran out of the park as fast as they could. They ran down side streets and back alleys. They kept running until the city streets became country roads.

Flora pointed at a barn in the distance. "Look," she said, "we could hide in there tonight."

"Good idea," said Bert.

It was almost midnight when Bert and Flora made two beds in a pile of hay.

"What a night," said Bert sleepily. "That was almost a disaster."

"I know," Flora said with a yawn. Then she remembered. "I forgot the money! We made a *lot* of money selling tickets, and I left it *all* in the park. Now we have *nothing*."

Bert jumped up. "That's not true. You still have two cents, don't you?"

Flora nodded and blinked back tears.

"We have each other," said Bert softly. "That's all that really matters."

"Hay," said Flora. "A barn."

"Exactly!" said Bert, snapping two of his claws. "A barn filled with hay suggests we're on a farm. And do you know what farms usually have?"

Flora shook her head.

"Chickens!" said Bert. "And where there are chickens, there are eggs. And where there are eggs, there are *scrambled* eggs."

"Breakfast," said Flora, grinning.

Bert nodded. "But first we have to get some sleep. Good night, Flora."

"Good night, Bert."

Bert and Flora fell asleep. They didn't know that two robbers named Buster and Robin were in the back of the barn with a bag containing $100,010.

CHAPTER SIX

The next morning, Buster and Robin were up at sunrise.

"What's for breakfast?" Buster asked.

"Scrambled eggs, toast, and coffee," Robin answered. He was cooking on a small camp stove in the back stall of the barn.

The smell awoke Bert. He hadn't eaten a hot meal in six days.

"Something smells delicious," he said, stretching.

"Smells like home," Flora added groggily.

Bert and Flora stopped talking when they heard two gruff voices discussing money.

"Me, too," said Buster. "Even when we divide the money in half, it'll still be a lot of cash. Let's see, half of one hundred thousand ten dollars is . . ." He paused to look for a pencil and paper.

Bert's eyes grew wide. "One hundred thousand ten dollars?" he whispered to Flora.

"Who *are* they?" Flora whispered back.

Bert held up one paw and then scampered over the hay pile to have a look.

He saw Robin cooking eggs in a skillet while Buster struggled with a math problem.

"Half of one hundred thousand ten dollars is . . ." Buster began again. "Well, let's see. This should be easy for a smart fella like me. All I have to do is, um—now don't tell me. I take the big number and put it here. Then I take the *whatchamacallit* and put it here."

Bert couldn't help himself. He tumbled down the hay and grabbed the pencil from Buster. "All you have to do is divide it by two. Here, watch me."

$100,000 ÷ 2 = $50,000
$10 ÷ 2 = $5
The answer is $50,005.

"Who are you?" asked Buster, scowling.

"Bert's my name. Pleasure to meet you. And now that I've answered *two* of your questions, may I ask one?"

"I suppose that's fair," said Buster, tearing off a corner of toast and stuffing it into his mouth.

"My question is this," said Bert. "How did you fine gentlemen come into possession of so much money?"

"Now *that's* a good story," Robin bragged as he dished up the scrambled eggs.

"Do tell," said Bert, helping himself to a tiny nibble of Buster's toast.

"Well, it was like this," Robin began. "A little girl ran away from home. Her mother is a bigwig captain on a ship who married some dude who worked in a circus."

Bert choked on the toast. "You don't say?"

"I *do* say," said Robin. "They put up a reward for the missing girl. One hundred thousand ten dollars. It was all the money they had in the world."

"And we stole it!" said Buster, stealing the punch line.

"Oh my," said Bert. His head was spinning. "What about the little girl? What about the ship captain and the man from the circus?"

"What about them?" said Robin with a careless shrug. "They'll probably never find their daughter. Guess that means they'll all live unhappily ever after. Ha!" As he laughed at his mean joke, bits of scrambled egg mixed with toast crumbs clung to the crusty corners of his mouth.

Bert's eyes suddenly filled with tears. "That's the saddest story I've ever heard."

"Oh, don't be a crybaby," said Buster. He swaggered over to the bag of reward money and pulled out a handful of dollars for Bert. "Here. Buy yourself a wheel of cheese."

Bert threw the dollars back at Buster. "I don't *want* your stolen money."

"Well, *I* do," said Flora.

There she was, standing in front of them with her hands on her hips.

"Who are *you*?" asked Buster.

Flora took a business card from her pocket and handed it to the men.

"You know me as the little girl who ran away from home," said Flora.

"That's *you*?" asked Buster and Robin at the same time.

"That's me," confirmed Flora. "And *this* is mine." She reached down and grabbed the bag of money.

In an instant, Buster and Robin were on their feet.

Buster and Robin chased Flora around the barn. Buster tried to karate chop the bag of money from her hands, but he couldn't. He kept tripping over the odd rake and garden hose that Bert was pushing into his path.

"Get the mouse!" Buster yelled at Robin. "Use your boot to *stomp* him!"

Robin ran after Bert. With every step, his heavy boots came dangerously close to crushing the small mouse.

"Hey, watch it, Mister Bigfoot!" said Bert, taking cover under a bucket. He paused to catch his breath.

Things were happening so fast. Bert tried to wrap his brain around it all. The thought of Captain LaPasta and Barnabas Brambles offering every dollar they had for Flora made his heart break. Bert wondered if anyone had bothered looking for him. *Do they even miss me?*

He remembered his sister, Gert. She was always so kind and clever. She could make up a new word to fit any occasion. Bert sighed. Gert would *never* have gotten herself into a mess like this. If she did, she'd have known how to get *out* of it.

Just then Bert heard Buster cackle with delight.

Ha! I've got her!
Little girls shouldn't steal money.
You're the thieves. That money was supposed to be a reward. Why don't you take me home now? Then the money will be yours.

"We can't do that," said Robin. "They'd throw us in jail for stealing. You don't think this is the first time we've pulled a stunt like this, do you? This is the way we roll. Hey, I just had a good idea."

"What?" said Buster.

"A kid could come in handy," said Robin. "We could use her to pull off our next robbery."

"The mouse might be helpful, too," said Buster. "With those little mitts, he'd be terrific for small jobs. Wonder if he could crack a safe with those claws."

Bert put his paws over his eyes and shook his head. This was bad. This was terrible. Pretending to be Squeaky was one thing. A life of crime was another. Once again, Bert's thoughts turned to his sister.

"What would Gert do right now?" Bert wondered aloud. As soon as he asked the question, he knew the answer: Gert would make up a word.

Bert popped out from under the bucket and whistled. "Hey, fellas!" he yelled. "Important question. Over here, please!"

Buster and Robin moved toward him as requested. Buster was holding Flora tightly by the hands. Robin carried the bag of money.

"I bet you guys have never seen a *mouscape*," Bert said casually.

"Huh?" said Buster.

"I've never even heard of a *mouscape*," said Robin. "What is it?"

"Well, now *that's* a good story," said Bert. "But you'd better sit down. It's a long story."

"We don't have time for this," Buster complained.

"Sure you do," Bert said. "Let go of Flora's hands so she can fluff up some hay into a pillow. You'll want to be comfortable while you listen."

Buster eyed Bert suspiciously. He wasn't sure he trusted the talking mouse, but he liked the idea of a hay pillow. He let go of Flora's hands.

Now,
a *mouscape* is
an interesting
creature.

"Sounds like a moose," said Buster.

"Sounds like something that wears a cape," added Robin.

"Excellent guesses," said Bert, "but incorrect. You see, a *mouscape* is not a moose. Nor does it have anything to do with a cape. A *mouscape,* you see, is . . ."

As Bert spoke, he slowly began untying the men's shoelaces. Buster and Robin were too engrossed in what Bert was saying to notice. Robin even let go of the money bag.

Flora could see what Bert was up to. She struggled to keep her smile from stretching across her entire face. "I would love to see a *mouscape*," she said, trying to sound serious.

"If you're lucky, you *will*," said Bert, raising his eyebrows at Flora. Together, Bert and Flora began tying the men's shoelaces in knots.

"Is a *mouscape* big or small?" asked Buster, paying no attention to his shoelaces.

"Is it dangerous?" asked Robin. "Does it bite?"

"It *could* bite," said Bert, "if it wanted to. But a *mouscape* prefers to use its brain. It's a terribly clever creature. Some say it's the cleverest creature in all of nature."

"We should steal one," Buster said to Robin.

"We could buy one," Robin replied. "We have plenty of money."

"Oh, but you can't buy a *mouscape,*" said Bert, wagging one claw at the robbers. The claw looked like a tiny windshield wiper. "You just have to be lucky enough to *see* one in the wild."

He and Flora were almost finished. Flora pulled the laces to form tight knots. The men still didn't notice.

"Too bad," grumbled Buster. "I really wanted to see a *mouscape.*"

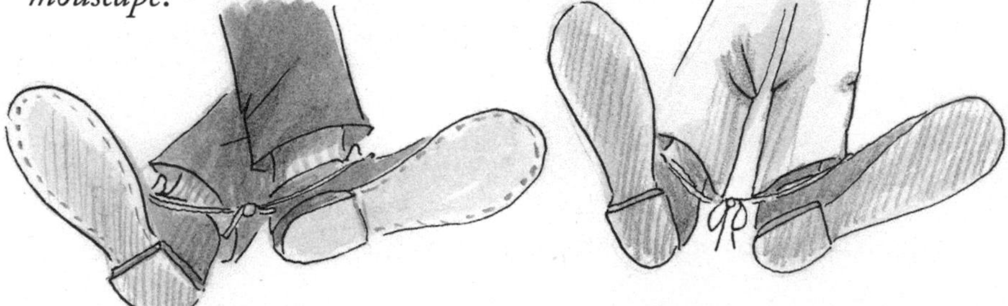

"Me, too," said Robin. "I'd give anything to see a *mouscape*."

Bert stepped away from the shoes. "Well, gentlemen, if it's a *mouscape* you want to see, watch closely." He turned to Flora. "Ready?"

"Ready," she said. She grabbed the bag of money for the second time and started to run. "Come on, Bert!"

"I'm right behind you!" he yelled.

The astonished men tried to get up, but they tripped and fell right back down. The harder they tried to stand, the more quickly they fell. They finally collapsed on top of each other in the hay.

You little sneaks!
What kind of dirty trick was that?

Bert answered over his shoulder as he ran. "You said you wanted to see a *mouscape*. You just did!"

Bert couldn't resist posting two signs on the barn.

Flora and Bert ran for miles. It was dark when they arrived at a railroad crossing.

"Where are we?" asked Bert, panting.

"I have no idea," said Flora, looking around.

A freight train appeared in the distance. It pulled into the station and stopped. The conductor jumped off the train. The stationmaster joined him on the platform.

"Anything serious?" the stationmaster asked.

"No," said the conductor, holding a flashlight so he could see what was wrong. "Minor mechanical problem, but it'll take me half the night to fix it."

Flora and Bert hid behind a tree and listened.

"Look," said Bert, pointing to the end of the train. "Do you see the last boxcar? The one that's not completely closed? If we squeeze through the gap, we could sleep inside the train tonight."

Bert and Flora crawled into the crowded boxcar and made beds from the cargo. The bags were surprisingly comfortable, but Flora and Bert couldn't sleep. They were hungry, hot, and dusty. They were also beginning to feel something else.

“It was a mistake to run away,” said Flora. “I had a nice home and parents who loved me. Now I have *nothing*.”

Bert used his nose to gesture to the bag of reward money. “You have one hundred thousand ten dollars and two cents.”

“I don’t care about money,” said Flora glumly. “Besides, that money isn’t mine. It belongs to my parents.”

“Well then,” said Bert, “you have *me*.”

Flora sniffled. “You’re sweet, Bert. You’re my best friend in the whole world. But I miss my mother. I miss Barnabas Brambles. I miss being *home*.”

Then you should go home.
I can’t.

“Why not?”

“Think how mad my mom is right now,” said Flora. “She would never forgive me for all the trouble I caused by running away.”

Bert nodded silently. He couldn't go home, either, for the exact opposite reason. He caused trouble when he *was* home. After all, he didn't clear the dinner table. He ignored his bath time. He had refused to clean up popcorn after the Minneapolis show. *Why?* Because he didn't feel like doing it. Oh, what he wouldn't give for some circus popcorn now!

For the first time since his balloon ride, it occurred to Bert that he might never see Sir Sidney again. Or any of his friends. Or his sister. His eyes filled with hot tears.

"At least somebody *misses* you," Bert cried. "Nobody misses me. Why hasn't Sir Sidney sent Old Coal to find me? That crow can find anyone in the whole wide world. There's only one logical explanation: They don't *want* to find me. They're *glad* I'm gone."

Oh, Bert, don't you know that everyone loved you?
Loved? You talk about me like I'm *dead.*

"Well, we could've died today," said Flora. "Those robbers were dangerous. So was Veronica Twist. Honestly, I don't know how much longer we can survive like this."

"Me, neither," Bert said.

A dreary rain began to fall. The steady thumping of heavy raindrops on the steel roof of the boxcar added another layer of gloom.

Flora and Bert lay in silence. Neither one could think of any words that would help the other feel better.

When the train began moving again at three o'clock in the morning, Flora and Bert didn't talk about where they might be heading. They just worried silently, unaware that they were on an express train filled with popcorn. It was on its way to make a very special delivery.

POP GOES the
Ci
us

DEPARTURES
GOURMET
POPCORN
THE CIRCUS TIMES
Funeral Planned for Circus Mouse

"We cover circus news like a tent!"

Saturday, August 2 **50 cents**

Polly Pumpkinseed, Publisher

Morning Edition

Funeral Planned for Circus Mouse

A funeral for Bert the circus mouse will be held tomorrow morning at eleven o'clock in the chapel at Sir Sidney's private peanut farm in Sidneyville, Ga. A popcorn reception will follow the funeral.

The missing mouse is presumed dead.

CHAPTER SEVEN

No one wanted to have a funeral for Bert. But after searching high and low for him without success, everyone in Sir Sidney's Circus agreed they should honor Bert's memory with a formal service.

The funeral attracted a big crowd. Friends, family, and fans came from all over the world for the sad event.

Barnabas Brambles arrived with Captain LaPasta. They walked slowly into the church, weeping quietly for Bert and his circus family. They cried for their own family, too, because they had hoped to find their daughter with Sir Sidney's Circus. But Flora wasn't there.

The clock atop the chapel tolled eleven times.

"It's eleven o'clock," Leo whispered sadly to Sir Sidney.

Sir Sidney nodded. "I'm just waiting for the popcorn delivery. The train should've been here hours ago."

"I'm sure the popcorn will arrive in time for the reception," said Sir Sidney. "Let's begin the funeral now. Waiting won't make it any easier."

The service began with a procession. Old Coal held a bouquet of flowers in her beak as she flew in solemn swoops down the aisle. Everyone else in Sir Sidney's Circus followed, each carrying a favorite picture of Bert.

Then Elsa performed a dance dedicated to Bert.

The Famous Flying Banana Brothers were next. They told the mourners that of all their routines, Bert had always loved their pineapple-upside-down-cakewalk trick best. They did a respectful version of it from the rafters of the chapel.

Next up were Leo and Tiger. They sang one of Bert's favorite songs.

If you need a friend
Who will stick with you
till the end,
Take my advice:
Get to know some mice.

The train arrived in the middle of the song. Workers flung open the boxcar doors and began unloading the bags of popcorn.

"Come on!" hollered one man to the rest of the crew. "We need to move all this popcorn to the garden. That's where they're having the popcorn reception."

Bert used his teeth to rip open a bag of buttery popcorn. He and Flora ate hungrily for several minutes before hopping off the train. No one saw them.

At first, Bert didn't know where he was. He had never seen the chapel at Sir Sidney's private peanut farm. He was surprised to hear familiar music coming from inside the small church.

"That's one of my favorite songs," Bert said, still chewing popcorn. "It always puts me in a good mood. Somebody must be getting married today."

"That's no wedding," said Flora, looking at the long black car parked in front of the chapel. "That's a funeral."

Bert stopped chewing. "What's a *funeral*?"

"It's when people get together after someone dies," Flora explained. "They tell stories and remember the good times they had together."

"Hmm," said Bert, mildly curious. "Shall we take a peek?"

The door creaked as Bert and Flora slipped inside the back of the chapel.

Leo and Tiger had just finished their song. Bert nearly jumped out of his fur when he saw them. "Good grief!" he squeaked.

"Shhh," whispered Flora. "Talking isn't allowed during funerals. We can only listen until it's over." Flora crouched behind a flower arrangement. Bert climbed up on her shoulder to get a better view.

They watched as Sir Sidney placed a comforting hand on Gert's back. It was his signal for her to begin.

Gert approached the podium. She was carrying a tiny scroll.

"Looks like Gert is going to make a speech," Bert whispered to Flora. "I wonder what she's going to say."

Flora put a finger to her lips.

"*Shhh,*" she reminded him.

Bert yawned. He was glad to see his sister, but he could never stay awake during a boring speech.

"He loved to laugh," Gert said sadly. "He was silly and funny. He enjoyed jokes and comic books. He was a devoted member of our circus and the best brother in the whole world. I don't know how I'm going to live without him." Tears were flowing from her small black eyes.

Bert's ears perked up and his eyes opened wide. "Good gosh!" he whispered to Flora. "She's talking about me. Is this *my* funeral?"

Flora nodded wordlessly. Her eyes were even wider than Bert's.

Gert continued to read from her prepared speech. "My brother wasn't always reliable," she said. "But I now realize that was one of his finest qualities. Bert was unpredictable. You just never knew what he was going to do next."

Bert nodded. "That's true," he whispered to himself.

Gert choked back sobs. "I know I speak for everyone in Sir Sidney's Circus when I say how hard it's been to close our business. But without Bert, there can be no circus."

Bert couldn't believe it. They had closed the circus because of *him*?

Gert was still talking. "It's true that Bert was small, but he was enormously important. And he was loved by everyone, especially me."

Now the whole congregation was crying. Even Sir Sidney was crying. Even *Bert* was crying. He couldn't remain silent one second longer.

Bert wiped his eyes, slid down Flora's arm, and landed on the floor. He brushed himself off. Then he stood up straight and began whistling in the back of the chapel.

First one mourner turned to look and then another. Soon everyone was transfixed. The mouse they had believed *dead* was walking down the aisle and *whistling*!

People gasped in disbelief. Mice wailed with happiness. An elderly elephant nearly collapsed from shock.

Bert held his head high. He was so proud, he felt as if he could fly. Instead, he started to sing.

(Sing to the tune of "Oh! Susanna" by Stephen Foster)

I come from Alabama
With a bandage on my knee.
I'm going to sing a little song,
So listen now to me.

I flew all night the day I left,
A strong wind carried me.
But then I heard a *POP* and I
Fell tail first in a tree.

(Chorus)
Oh! Sir Sidney,
Oh don't you cry for me,
'Cause I'm back today from far away,
Alive as I can be.

I met two men the other day.
I found them near some hay.
One chased me with his heavy boots,
But it turned out okay.

The day before was worse, I'd say,
'Cause I was in a play.
It ended bad;
The crowd got mad.
Thank gosh I got away!

No one could believe their eyes or ears. Gert ran to Bert and flung her paws around him joyfully. Immediately, her gray fur started to turn brown again. The other members of the circus surrounded Bert in an enormous group hug. Elsa used her trunk to raise him over their heads like a trophy.

Bert laughed, his eyes still glistening with tears. "And guess what? I'm not the only one who's back today!" He pointed to the back of the chapel.

Tears of happiness streamed down Captain LaPasta's cheeks.

Flora was shocked to see her mother and Barnabas Brambles. As she ran to meet them, she sang the final chorus of Bert's song.

"My darling Flora," said Captain LaPasta, covering her daughter with kisses. "This is the most *wonderful* surprise!"

"It gets better," said Flora. She showed her mother the bag of reward money.

"Where on earth did you get it?" Captain LaPasta asked.

"Now *that's* a good story," said Flora, winking at Bert. "I'll tell you all about it later."

"Please do," said Barnabas Brambles. "Meanwhile, we have a little surprise for you." He moved so Flora could see what her mother was holding: a baby.

"He's just two days old," Captain LaPasta told Flora.

Would you like to hold your brother?
Yes.

Flora had never held a baby before. She was surprised by how light he was. She didn't know a baby could smell so sweet, almost like freshly baked bread.

"What's his name?" Flora asked.

Captain LaPasta laughed. "We haven't had time to think of a name. We were too busy looking for you." She paused. "But *I* was thinking—"

"And I was thinking," interrupted Barnabas Brambles.

The baby should have my name.
The baby should have my name.

"Great!" said Bert. "You can call him Barnabas LaPasta—or Barney for short."

Everyone agreed it was the perfect name for the baby.

"What do you think the baby will call *me*?" asked Barnabas Brambles.

Just then the baby opened his eyes and made a noise. It sounded exactly like:

"It's high time we celebrate all this wonderful news," said Sir Sidney. "Please join me in the garden for a popcorn reception in honor of Bert, Flora, and baby Barney."

The jolly crowd began to head out of the chapel.

"Old Coal," said Gert, "please bring your bouquet to the reception. I'll find a pretty vase for the flowers."

"Aw! Aw!" answered Old Coal. The black bird flew toward the chapel door, but she misjudged the distance. She hit her beak on the door and fell to the ground.

"Old Coal," said Sir Sidney gently, "lately you've had trouble judging distances. You've also had a lot of headaches. I was wondering why you couldn't find Bert. Now I think I know."

"Aw?" whimpered Old Coal.

Sir Sidney removed his glasses and placed them on the crow's beak. Immediately, she perked up and flew around the chapel twice. Then she swooped down to lovingly peck Sir Sidney on the cheek. Her headache was gone!

Sir Sidney laughed. "You can wear my glasses the rest of the day, Old Coal. We'll get you a pair tomorrow. Now let's all go enjoy some popcorn, shall we?"

CHAPTER EIGHT

It was hard for Flora and Bert to say good-bye. After their exciting adventure, they knew they'd be friends for life. But they also knew where they each belonged: *home.*

What's better than running away from home?
Going back home. That's my two cents' worth, anyway.
You've always had good sense.
Most girls do.

For Flora, returning to the SS *Spaghetti* with Barney meant she was never lonely or bored.

She discovered she liked feeding her baby brother.

She enjoyed reading to him.

She didn't even mind changing his diapers . . .

or assembling the new crib.

But what Flora enjoyed most of all was trying to make Barney laugh.

Welcome Aboard to Our New Baby
Barnabas Banana Susanna Sir Sidney LaBuena LaPasta
Born: August 1
Weight: 7 pounds
First word: Pop!

Back on the circus train, everyone was offering to help Bert with his chores.

Well, it wasn't fun. Not for Bert, anyway.

"Chores are a bore," he grumbled as he began to clear the dinner table. He tried to make the task more fun by turning one plate on its side and running on top of it to move it across the table.

Gert watched her brother. Bert had been gone only a week, but to Gert it had seemed a lifetime. "Please promise me you'll never run away again," she said.

Bert hopped off the plate. "But I didn't run away, Gert. I got carried away by a balloon. It was the most exciting thing that's ever happened to me!"

He thought back to his remarkable journey. How terrified he'd felt hanging on to the balloon for dear life. How scary it was when the balloon popped. How exciting it had been to find

Flora. How funny it was when they pretended to be Veronica Twist and

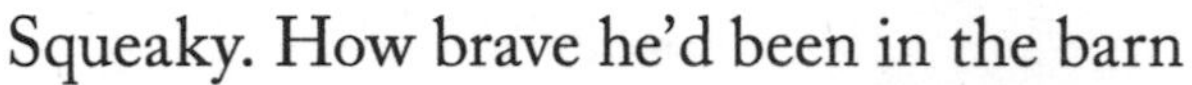

Squeaky. How brave he'd been in the barn

with the two robbers. Or was it really a bit *reckless* of him to have tricked those scoundrels with

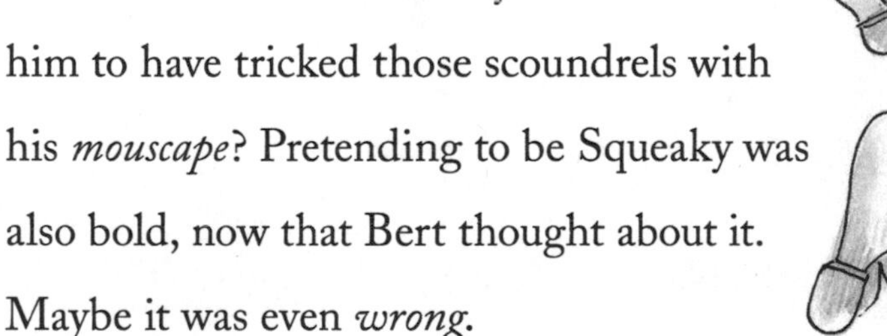

his *mouscape*? Pretending to be Squeaky was also bold, now that Bert thought about it. Maybe it was even *wrong*.

The more Bert thought about his adventure, the less he wanted to tell Gert everything that had happened.

"The thing is," said Bert, rubbing his chin, "if you don't mind, I'd like to *think* about my adventure before I tell you about it."

Gert smiled. "Are you saying you now have some deep thoughts and thrilling secrets? Maybe your adventure even included some exciting tidbits?"

Bert nodded. He couldn't remember where he'd heard those phrases before. That's when Gert handed him the pocket-size diary he'd left behind.

Bert turned the blank book over in his paws. "This is exactly what I need," he said. "But there's a big problem."

"What?" said Gert.

"I can't *possibly* fit everything that happened to me in this tiny book. I'm going to need at least *two* diaries. Maybe three. There's so much to write!"

"If you finish one diary," said Gert, "I'm sure Sir Sidney will give you another."

Later that night, Sir Sidney was putting the finishing touches on a poster.

An Important Message
from Sir Sidney's Circus
We are so happy Bert is back home.
Our business will reopen soon.
Our next show will be

Sir Sidney put down his pen. He wondered whether Bert might want to rest a bit before the circus resumed full operations. The little mouse had certainly been through *a lot* lately. Sir Sidney decided to ask Bert.

Sir Sidney found Gert instead. "I'm looking for your brother. Do you know where he is?"

"I do," said Gert.

She led Sir Sidney to the mouse hole and suggested he look inside.

They leaned in close to listen. They could hear Bert laughing as his pencil scratched across the pages of his diary. As usual, Bert's tail twitched every time he laughed.

Sir Sidney smiled. "I think we have a writer on our hands."

Bert had a *gladitude,* too. Sure, it was wonderful to be a writer. But it was even more wonderful to know that when he was gone, he was missed. He was loved by everyone in the circus, even though he was unpredictable. *Life* was unpredictable! Maybe that's why it felt so good to be home.

This, Bert thought, *is the best day of my life.*

He closed his eyes and held on tightly to that thought, like it was a balloon that could take him anywhere.

THE
END
But I'll have *a lot* more to tell you later!

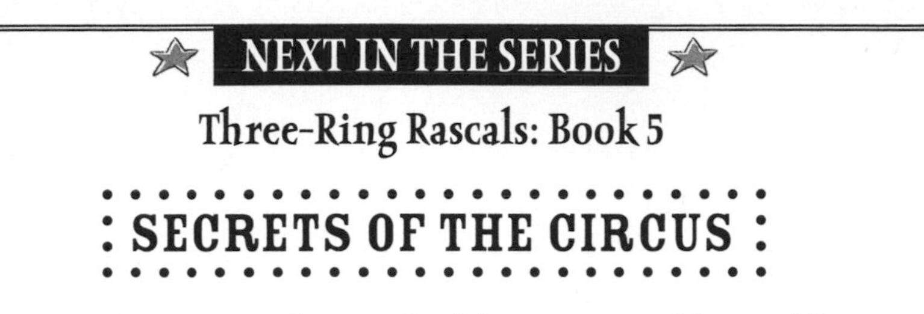

NEXT IN THE SERIES
Three-Ring Rascals: Book 5
SECRETS OF THE CIRCUS

Everyone has a secret. So says Sir Sidney, owner of the world's best circus. But sometimes a little secret can become a **BIG** problem.

That's **EXACTLY** what happens when Gert's secret pen pal, a pig named Pablo, escapes from his farm and climbs aboard the circus train. Gert can't bear the thought of her friend becoming pork chops. Sir Sidney agrees, but he also feels sorry for Farmer Farley, who must sell Pablo to save the farm.

When **EVERYONE**, including Farmer Farley, reads in the *New Pork Times* about a pig **RACE** at the Iowa State Fair with a $5,000 prize, it's no secret where the whole gang will meet.

See you at the pig race! Who will win? Who will cry? Who will take home the biggest secret of all? Find out in

SECRETS OF THE CIRCUS.

You won't be *boared.*

ABOUT THE AUTHOR AND ILLUSTRATOR

KATE KLISE and **M. SARAH KLISE** are sisters who like to write (Kate) and draw (Sarah). They began making books when they were little girls who shared a bedroom in Peoria, Illinois. Kate now lives and writes in an old farmhouse on forty acres in the Missouri Ozarks. Sarah draws and dwells in a Victorian cottage in Berkeley, California. Together the Klise sisters have created more than twenty award-winning books for young readers. Their goal always is to make the kind of fun-to-read books they loved years ago when they were kids.

To learn more about the Klise sisters, visit their website: www.kateandsarahklise.com.

You might also enjoy visiting Sir Sidney and his friends at www.threeringrascals.com.

REWARD!
Flora Endora Eliza LaBuena LaPasta
If you have any information about this girl,
please contact the SS Spaghetti.
$100,010 reward offered.
ONE TICKET
Veronica Twist the Ventriloquist
and her sidekick Squeaky
Ticket price: $3
Have You Seen This Mouse?
Bert the Mouse
Our beloved friend is gone.
Please help us find him.
Contact Sir Sidney's Circus.
Bert's Chores
~Clean up popcorn
after every show
~Clear table after dinner
~Write in diary